Poles Apart

Celia Warren
Illustrated by Mike Terry

Walrus lived on the cold ice at the North Pole.

One day Walrus said, "I would love to go and see my friend Penguin."

So Walrus left his home and set off on the long journey to the South Pole.

Penguin lived on the cold ice at the South Pole.

On the very same day Penguin said, "I would love to go and see my friend Walrus."

So Penguin left her home and set off on the long journey to the North Pole.

Walrus had not gone far when he met some huskies. They took him for a ride in a sleigh. Walrus was so excited that he sent a postcard to Penguin.

Dear Penguin,
 I am on my way to visit you.
 Today I went for a ride in a sleigh.
 I can't wait to see you.
Love,
Walrus

Penguin
South Pole

Meanwhile, Penguin was in Australia. She met some friendly kangaroos. They showed her how to jump. Penguin was so excited that she sent a postcard to Walrus.

Dear Walrus,
   I am on my way to visit you.
   I am having fun jumping with the kangaroos.
   I will see you soon.
Love,
Penguin

Walrus
North Pole

Meanwhile, Walrus swam and swam until he came to Hawaii. He met some people on the beach. They put a garland of flowers around his neck and showed him how to dance.

Walrus couldn't wait to tell Penguin, so he sent her a postcard.

Meanwhile, Penguin travelled on. She came to China. She saw a wonderful firework display and a dancing dragon. Penguin sent Walrus a postcard.

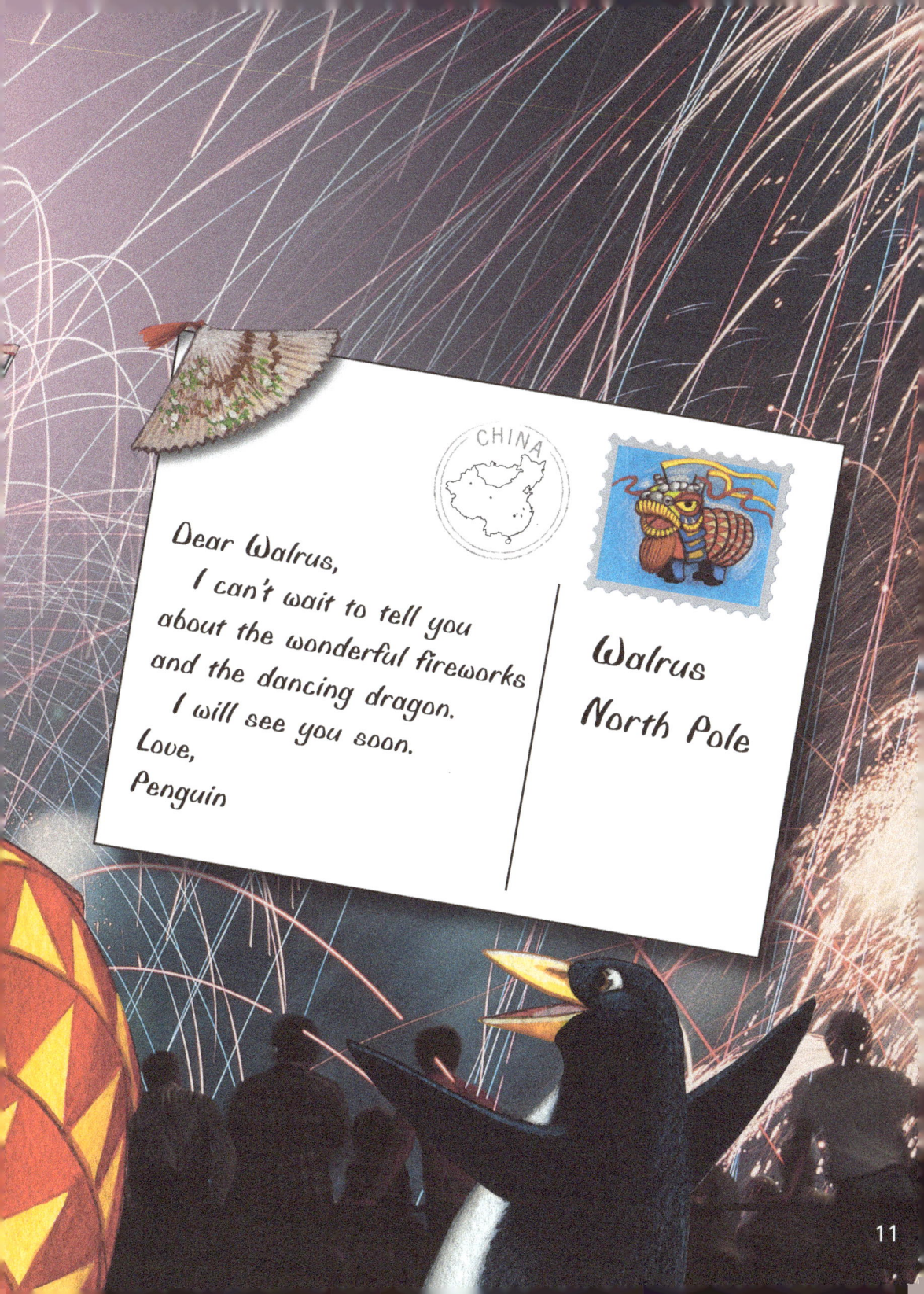

Dear Walrus,
 I can't wait to tell you about the wonderful fireworks and the dancing dragon.
 I will see you soon.
Love,
Penguin

Walrus
North Pole

Walrus came to a rain forest in Brazil, where he met a parrot.
"I am too hot," said Walrus.
"I am too hot," said the parrot.
"I miss my nice ice," said Walrus.
"I miss my nice ice," said the parrot.
"Good-bye," said Walrus.
"Good-bye," said the parrot.
Walrus sent a postcard to Penguin.

Dear Penguin,
 I am in a hot rain forest with a talking parrot.
 I wish you were here!
 I miss my nice ice and I can't wait to see you.
Love,
Walrus

Penguin

South Pole

Walrus and Penguin travelled over land and sea until they came to Egypt.

Walrus went to look at the pyramids.
Penguin went to look at the pyramids.
Then they met!
"Walrus, it's you!" laughed Penguin.
"Penguin, it's you!" laughed Walrus.
They were so happy to see each other.

Then they had some adventures together. They had a ride on a train – a camel train!

They visited a museum.
Walrus learned another dance.

After that, to cool off, they had a ride down the River Nile.

"This is the life," said Penguin.

"This is the life," said Walrus.

Soon, it was time to say good-bye. Walrus wanted to go home to the North Pole. Penguin wanted to go home to the South Pole.

"I miss my nice ice," said Walrus.

"Me too," said Penguin.

Walrus went home to the North Pole. "What a lot of postcards from Penguin!" he said. He sent another postcard to Penguin.

Dear Penguin
It was good to see you.
I hope you got home safely.
See you again soon.
Love,
Walrus
P.S. I miss you — but it's nice to be home!

Penguin
South Pole

Penguin went home to the South Pole. "What a lot of postcards from Walrus," she said. She sent another postcard to Walrus.

Dear Walrus,
 This is the first time that I have been half-way around the world, but I hope it will not be the last!
 We may be poles apart, but we're the best of friends!
Love, Penguin

Walrus
North Pole